To Ryan.

Yahoo!

Eric A. Kimmel
·1991·

CHARLIE DRIVES

THE STAGE

BY **ERIC A. KIMMEL**

ILLUSTRATED BY **GLEN ROUNDS**

HOLIDAY HOUSE / NEW YORK

Library of Congress Cataloging-in-Publication Data

Kimmel, Eric A.
Charlies drives the stage / written by Eric A. Kimmel; illustrated
by Glen Rounds. — 1st ed.
p.   cm.
Summary: Neither avalanche, nor Indians, nor flooding river can
keep a daring young stagecoach driver from delivering Senator
McCorkle to the train station on time.
ISBN 0-8234-0738-1
[1. Coaching—Fiction.   2. West (U.S.)—Fiction.]   I. Rounds,
Glen. 1906-   ill.   II. Title.
PZ7.K5648Ci   1989
[E]—dc19   88-24558   2   CIP   AC

ISBN 0-8234-0738-1

For Barb *and* Tom

On Tuesday morning at eight o'clock a stranger walked into the Grass Valley office of the Overland Stagecoach Company.

"When does the next stage leave for La Grande?" he asked. "I have to catch the five o'clock train."

Pete Parker, the ticket agent, laughed in his face. "You're outta luck, Mister. There ain't no next stage to La Grande. There ain't no next stage nowhere. Not today, not tomorrow. Might not be one for another week. Ain't you heard? There's avalanches in the pass, road agents on the road, and Indians on the warpath. On top of that the river's rising and the bridge is most likely out. If you wanna go to La Grande, you're gonna hafta fly. Ain't that right, boys?"

The three drivers playing cards at the table nodded. "That's right, Pete," they said.

The stranger put his nose up close to Pete's. "Do you have any idea who I am?"

"Can't say as I do."

"Does the name Roscoe McCorkle mean anything to you?"

"Sure does! He's that fancy senator visiting from back East. I read about him in the newspaper."

"Well, I happen to be Senator McCorkle, and I have a very important meeting in Washington on Friday with the president. It is essential that I be there, that is, unless you don't really care if this territory of yours becomes a state."

Three hands of cards dropped on the table. Every head in the room turned.

"Jumping Jerusalem! That puts a new face on things, don't it." Pete reached out to shake hands with the stranger. "I don't know what to tell you, Senator. How about it, boys? Think one of you can make it to La Grande?"

The drivers picked up their cards at once.

"No, sir!"

"I ain't risking my neck."

"Or my hair."

"You see how it is," Pete Parker said. "They're scared. I don't blame them. There's only one driver with a ghost of a chance of getting through. That's Charlie Drummond."

"Where do I find this Charlie Drummond?"

"Over at the library, I expect, reading a book. Charlie sure has some mighty strange notions."

The senator walked down the street to the library. "I'm looking for Charlie Drummond," he told the librarian.

"Shhhhh!" She pointed to a sign on her desk:

LOUD TALKING AND

GUNS NOT PERMITTED

"Sorry," the senator whispered.

"Charlie's over there." The librarian pointed out a small, feisty-looking fellow in a buckskin jacket sitting in a chair against the wall. He was wearing a wide-brimmed hat pinned up in front and reading *Little Women*. Senator McCorkle thought that was strange.

"Charlie Drummond?" he asked.

Charlie looked up. His smooth sunburned face and clear blue eyes were not at all what the senator expected. Unlike the other drivers, he didn't have whiskers. He looked about fourteen years old.

"I'm Senator McCorkle, son. I have to be in La Grande by five o'clock to catch a train for Washington. They tell me you're the only one who can get me there on time."

Charlie thought it over. "Well, I'll do my best. But you got to know something before we start. Once we get going, we don't stop. And we don't turn back. That okay with you?"

The senator nodded.

"Fine. Now you go have breakfast. I'll meet you at the stage office in an hour."

The senator was at the stage office an hour later. So was Charlie. He hitched up the four-horse team, lit a cigar, and climbed up to the driver's box. The senator took his seat inside. Charlie grasped the reins. "Look out, La Grande! Here we come!"

The stage picked up speed as it rolled out of town.

By noon they were heading into the mountains, climbing straight up on a road so narrow a cat would think twice about turning around. The senator cast a nervous glance out the window. Far below he saw a wild river boiling through a rocky gorge. Above his head snowy peaks pierced the clouds. He thought to himself, "I hope that driver knows what he's doing." Suddenly he heard a rumble like a herd of dinosaurs stirring. Looking up, he saw the whole side of the mountain beginning to slide.

"Great Cato's Granny!" Senator McCorkle yelped.

"It's an avalanche!" Charlie hollered back. "Hang on, Senator. I'm gonna make a run for it."

"You can't outrun an avalanche!"

"You can if you go fast enough! EEEYAH!!!"

The stagecoach plunged ahead. Poor Senator McCorkle bounced around like a fly in a churn as Charlie took the hairpin turns on two wheels. The rumble of grinding rock shook the mountains. Then it stopped.

"Whew! I guess we made it," said Charlie

Senator McCorkle shook all over like a calf at branding time.

"That's mighty fine driving, Charlie," he stammered, "but I was thinking. It might not be so bad if I missed that train. I could always telegraph the president I'll be late."

"Don't you worry about that, Senator," said Charlie. "I said I'd put you on that train, and I will."

They crossed the mountains uneventfully, if falling trees and boulders don't count as events. The road descended, following the river through a narrow, high-walled canyon.

"I don't like this place at all," Senator McCorkle declared as he looked out the window. "It strikes me as a good spot for an ambush."

Charlie agreed. "That's why they call it Ambush Canyon. Uh-oh! Keep your head down, Senator. We got company."

Four men on horseback suddenly appeared in the road ahead. They wore black bandannas across their faces and carried rifles.

"Stop that stage! Throw down your guns!" they ordered.

"Sorry boys! Can't stop to jaw with you. The senator has to catch the five o'clock train in La Grande. But how 'bout a smoke?" Charlie pulled out a stick of dynamite, lit the fuse with his cigar, and flung it at the outlaws. The explosion shattered the stagecoach windows. When the smoke cleared, the road agents were gone.

"Shucks!" laughed Charlie. "I gotta pay attention. I thought that was a cigar."

The senator picked shards of broken glass out of his hat. "You carry dynamite?"

"Sure do! It's great stuff. You never know when it'll come in handy."

Senator McCorkle crossed his fingers and started saying his prayers.

The river grew wilder as they rode along. Angry brown water surged against the banks, sweeping away trees, stumps, and boulders.

By now Senator McCorkle wished he'd never left Grass Valley. "Charlie, I think we better turn back while we still have the chance."

"You let me worry about that, Senator. I'm driving." Just then the senator noticed a thin column of smoke rising above the canyon. He saw another, then another, until he counted more than a dozen. Charlie saw them too. "Smoke signals."

"Smoke signals? That means . . . !"

". . . Indians. But don't you worry, Senator. All the Indians in these parts are friends of mine."

A flight of arrows struck the stagecoach. One went through Charlie's hat.

"Holy Hannah! They must not be from around here."

"Look out!" Senator McCorkle yelled as hundreds of Indians swarmed into the canyon.

"Don't worry, Senator. It's only a mile to the bridge. We'll make a stand on the other side once we get across."

"What if we don't get across? What if they catch us? What if the bridge is out?"

Charlie lit another cigar. "You got to think positive about these things, Senator."

The stagecoach tore down the road with the Indians close behind. Within a few minutes the bridge appeared. It looked none too sturdy. The plank roadway wobbled back and forth as the surging river tore at its pilings.

"It's breaking up! Turn back, Charlie! We'll never get across! I can't look." Senator McCorkle covered his eyes.

By now the stagecoach was stuck with so many arrows it looked like the main target at an archery contest. Charlie drove straight on.

"Hold on, Senator! She's gonna hit!"

An enormous tree washed down by the river struck the bridge with battering ram force. Timbers cracked, nails groaned, planks splintered. The shattered bridge collapsed into the river. The current swept the wreckage away.

"Are we dead yet?" Senator McCorkle still had his eyes covered.

"Naw, we ain't dead. But it was close. You can look now."

They had made it across the bridge just in time. Glancing back, Senator McCorkle saw the Indians as tiny dots. The stagecoach rolled on.

"You can relax now, Senator. The worst is over. La Grande is just over that rise. We'll be there before you know it."

Senator McCorkle looked at his watch. He hoped Charlie was right. It was already 4:45.

Ten minutes later they drove into La Grande. People, dogs, and horses ran to get out of the way as the stagecoach tore down Main Street, heading for the railway station.

The train was gone.

Senator McCorkle dashed onto the platform. "This can't be! It's only 4:55!"

"You better set your watch, Mister!" the stationmaster told him. "It's 5:30. That train left here half an hour ago."

"Then do something! Telegraph ahead! Call it back! I'm Senator McCorkle, I tell you. The president wants me in Washington on Friday."

"I don't care if you're the king of Siam," the stationmaster said. "That train is gone."

Then Charlie spoke up. "Get back in the stage, Senator."

"What?"

"I said get back in the stage. I promised I'd put you on that train, didn't I? Well, let's not stand around wasting time."

With Senator McCorkle back inside, the stagecoach shot out of La Grande, its wheels smoking. Railroad tracks and telephone poles whizzed by. Soon they saw the smoke of an engine. Within a few minutes the train appeared.

"Haw! Git on there!" Charlie drove like a man with his pants on fire. They passed the caboose, the baggage car, the passenger cars. People on the train crowded to the windows

to see the stagecoach speed by. "It's Charlie Drummond!" someone yelled. "Three cheers for Charlie!" And everyone aboard the train shouted, "Hip, hip, hooray!"

They were running neck and neck with the engine now. The engineer pulled back on the throttle. "Charlie, what are you trying to do? Put me out of business?"

"Stop the train, Ed. I got another passenger for you."

The engineer blew the whistle. The train screeched to a halt in a great cloud of steam. Senator McCorkle got down from the stagecoach. As soon as the people on the train recognized their new fellow passenger, they gathered around to shake his hand. Senator McCorkle was glad to oblige.

"All aboard!" The conductor signaled to the engineer to start the engine.

The senator shook Charlie's hand.

"I won't forget this, son. As soon as I get back to Washington, I intend to tell the president about you. Expect to hear from me soon. I have big plans for you, Mister Charles Drummond."

The train began to move.

"Sure obliged, Senator. But I'm afraid you got the name wrong."

"Why, it is Drummond, isn't it?"

"Drummond's right. Charles ain't."

"But everyone calls you Charlie."

"That's true."

"Then I don't understand . . ."

The train picked up speed as it pulled away.

"Shoot, Senator! Didn't anyone in Grass Valley tell you?"

"Tell me what?"

"My name . . .

IT'S CHARLENE!!!"